Nine Lives

BEN M. BAGLIO

Nine Lives
Ginger, Nutmeg, and Clove

Illustrated by Bill Geldart

AN **APPLE** PAPERBACK

SCHOLASTIC INC.

New York Toronto London Auckland Sydney
Mexico City New Delhi Hong Kong Buenos Aires

ISBN 0-439-32256-1

12 11 10 9 8   2 3 4 5 6/0

Printed in the U.S.A.   40
First Scholastic printing, October 2001

For Lucy — a little cat with a big heart who is very much missed.

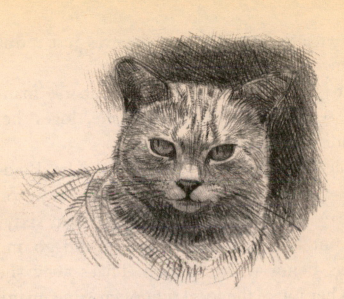

Nine Lives

Bracken is a large tortoiseshell cat that lives with the Bradman family on Liberty Street. Bracken lives a comfortable life and spends much of her time snoozing away in her basket in the Bradmans' house.

Mr. Bradman — Dad — used to be a lawyer, but he gave up this career for his real passion — gardening. He found Bracken abandoned in an alley two years ago when she was just a tiny kitten.

Mrs. Bradman — Mom — is a bank manager. Unlike Mr. Bradman, she loves her indoor office job.

Elsie Jennings — Grandma — is Mrs. Bradman's mom. She lives a few doors away on Liberty Street. She may be older than sixty-five, but Elsie has lots of get-up-and-go and enjoys being with children. That's why she loves her job as the local school crossing guard.

Tom Bradman is thirteen years old and has an early morning job as a paperboy. He and his younger sister, Ellie, love animals. They always make a big fuss over Bracken and their six-year-old golden retriever, Lottie.

Ellie Bradman is ten years old. She's always coming up with great plans and ideas — which is just as well . . . because earlier this year Bracken had her first litter. She became the proud mom of nine assorted bundles of fur.

Nine kittens, nine very different lives. The Bradmans know they can't keep the kittens, but they're determined that all nine go to the very best homes — homes to suit each very special personality.

Ginger

1

Ginger dashed across the garden and pounced. Oh, no! It was only a leaf. But when he lifted his paws, the leaf fluttered in the wind. Interesting. He pounced again. Another leaf whirled by. Ginger went after it.

He chased the leaf all the way to the fruit trees at the bottom of the yard, then scrambled up the trunk of an apple tree. By now, he was out of breath, but that didn't stop him. He was having too much fun!

Once he reached the top, Ginger clawed his way along a branch until it grew too thin to hold his weight. It began to bend and sway beneath him. For a moment, he held on, then dropped lightly to the ground, landing on all four paws in the soft grass.

Suddenly, a sharp bark made Ginger jump. It came from behind the hedge at the side of the garden. *But they don't have a dog next door,* Ginger thought. *So what's going on?* He decided he would go and find out. Ginger crept toward the hedge and pushed his nose through a gap. A split second later, he wished he hadn't!

Snap! A set of sharp teeth brushed just past his nose. Glaring down at him was a brown-and-white dog with a big, squashed nose.

"Get away!" hissed Ginger, ducking back into his own yard and bolting across the grass. He didn't look where he was going and bumped straight into Mr. Bradman, the gardener, who was pruning roses near the house.

"Don't be frightened," said Mr. Bradman, petting Ginger with one hand and rubbing his ankle with the other. "It's only a dog. You weren't scared of Lottie when you lived with us."

"But Lottie didn't try and bite my nose off!" meowed Ginger crossly.

Ginger had been born in Mr. Bradman's house on Liberty Street. Ginger's mom, Bracken, still lived there. It was Mr. Bradman who had found Ginger his new home with Amy and her mom.

"The dog's only visiting," said Mr. Bradman. "I saw it arrive with its owners a few minutes ago. But if you're always going to be so nosy, you're bound to have a few scrapes now and then."

"I can't help it," meowed Ginger. "I just like to know what's going on."

"You always were the daredevil of the litter!" laughed Mr. Bradman.

Ginger rolled over onto his back and Mr. Bradman tickled the cat's tummy. Being careful not to use his claws, Ginger grabbed Mr. Bradman's hand with his front paws. He didn't want to hurt him.

"You're becoming a fine young cat," said Mr. Bradman. "Look at the size of those paws. You'll be as big as a lion, I think, if you continue growing at this rate. And handsome, too. Such beautiful thick fur. No wonder you were one of the first in the litter to be picked."

"Thank you," purred Ginger.

"Nine months old, and almost as big as an adult cat already," said Mr. Bradman.

A robin landed on the wheelbarrow a few yards away. As quick as a flash, Ginger sprang. But he was not quick enough and the robin flew to the safety of a fence post. It twittered noisily at Ginger, but Ginger had lost interest already — he had just seen Amy and her mom coming through the gate.

Ginger loved both of them, but he especially

loved Amy. They had a lot of fun playing together. Amy and her mom lived in the upstairs apartment of Ms. Somers's house. Ms. Somers was a very kind lady. She looked after Amy and Ginger when Amy's mom worked. Amy's mom had to work all sorts of odd hours.

"Hello, Ginger," Amy said as he ran to meet her. She bent down and picked him up. Ginger wrapped his furry arms around her neck and almost got tangled up in her hair. "Did you miss me?" Amy asked.

"Yes," purred Ginger. "But I've had a few adventures, too!"

Ginger felt a bigger hand stroke his head. He turned and looked up. It was Amy's mom. She had the same twinkling blue eyes and long blond hair as Amy and she was the one who bought the cat food! Ginger gave her his cutest look.

"Mr. Bradman," said Amy. "Has Ginger been up to mischief again?"

"A little," laughed Mr. Bradman. "But it's hard to be angry with him. He's so lively!"

Ginger purred happily.

"Oh, look," said Amy. "There's Ms. Somers." She pointed toward the house. The white-haired lady was waving through the window. Amy waved back.

"She's so kind," said Amy's mom to Mr. Bradman. "And a wonderful landlady."

"And she baby-sits Ginger and me when Mom works nights," Amy said. "Doesn't she, Ginger?"

Ginger purred contentedly.

"And she won't take a penny for watching them," Amy's mom added. "I wish she would. I'm sure she could use a little more money."

"That's why I charge her less than my usual fee when I come and do the yard," said Mr. Bradman. "But you won't tell her that, will you?"

"Of course we won't," said Amy's mom.

"Anyway, pruning a few rosebushes is hardly landscape gardening, is it?" laughed Mr. Bradman.

Amy's mom looked at her watch. "Oh, dear, we must hurry up, Amy," she said. "I'm on the late shift tonight."

Amy put Ginger down and ran toward the house. "Come on, Ginger," she called. "Dinnertime!"

Ginger scampered after her, soon overtaking her and reaching the back door first. He stood with his front paws resting on the door, waiting for Amy and her mom to catch up. As soon as the door was open, he raced up the stairs and into the kitchen. "Hurry up," he meowed. "I'm starving!"

Ginger purred with delight as Amy filled his dish. As soon as Amy's elbow moved out of the way, he guzzled the entire contents of the dish in record time.

"You were hungry!" laughed Amy.

Ginger pushed his head against Amy's legs. "I'm still hungry," he meowed.

"You want more?!" said Amy. "You'll explode!"

But Ginger had no trouble finishing the second helping that Amy put into his dish.

Amy's mom had been preparing their meal. "He's a growing boy!" she said. "Ours is ready now, Amy."

"Coming!" said her daughter.

Amy left Ginger cleaning his whiskers. She washed her hands and went to sit at the table with her mom. While she ate her pizza, she watched Ginger. "He never sits still, does he?" she said. "Always investigating something."

At that moment, Ginger noticed a large, empty bag on the kitchen floor. As if to prove Amy right, he stalked around the bag, poked it, peered inside it, then jumped on it. But he soon grew bored with it and found a cardboard box in the corner instead. He jumped lightly over the side, sniffed around, chased his tail, then sat looking at Amy and her mom.

"I have to go," said Amy's mom. "I'm expected at work in half an hour. Ms. Somers is waiting for you."

They quickly did the dishes and got ready to go downstairs. Ginger stretched and sharpened his claws on the inside of the box, then leaped nimbly out of it. "I'm ready," he meowed.

"Come on, then," said Amy, and she carried him downstairs and knocked on Ms. Somers's door. Her mom was right behind them.

"Hello, Amy dear," said Ms. Somers. "I've taken out a board game this evening. I thought we could play before your bedtime."

Amy smiled — she enjoyed spending some of her evenings with Ms. Somers even though there was no television. Ms. Somers was an old-fashioned person, with her hair in a bun and her wire-rimmed glasses perched on the end of her nose, but she always found plenty of fun things for them to do.

Amy gave her mom a quick hug. "Bye, Mom," she said. "Be careful!"

Amy's mom nodded and then, smiling, closed the door behind her.

Ginger had gone to the window. He could see Mr. Bradman still outside in the yard. As he watched, Mr. Bradman disappeared into the shed. Ginger wondered what was in there. He thought it must be full of interesting things.

"Can I go out?" Ginger meowed.

Ms. Somers opened the window and let Ginger jump out. Mr. Bradman was coming out of the shed. Seeing Ginger running toward him, he stopped what he was doing and bent down to pet the kitten.

"I like coming out to see you," meowed Ginger.

"Hello again," said Mr. Bradman. "I'm just putting the tools back in the shed. It's time I went home for my dinner."

"I've had mine," meowed Ginger. "I ate two dishfuls."

A leaf blew past Ginger. He couldn't resist it and ran off across the yard after it.

An hour later, Ms. Somers glanced up at the clock.

"My goodness," she said. "It's past your bed-time. Your mom will be upset if she finds out how late we stayed up!"

Amy smiled. She liked being up later than

her bedtime. And anyway, her mom wouldn't mind because tomorrow was Saturday! But she nodded, then said, "We'd better call Ginger in. He shouldn't be out after dark."

They opened the back door and called. But Ginger didn't come. Amy wandered out into the yard. "Ginger!" She giggled nervously. "Stop playing games with us." *He usually always comes when he's called*, Amy thought.

She walked farther down, toward the fruit trees. "Ginger! Where are you?" she called. "Come on, boy."

Ms. Somers brought a flashlight from her kitchen and shone it under the bushes and up at the trees, but there was no sign of the ginger kitten.

Amy began to feel worried. *Suppose he's gone exploring and got lost? Or what if he's in some sort of danger?* "Come on, Ms. Somers," she said as she set off to search the whole yard again. "We've got to find him."

2

Amy and Ms. Somers hunted for a long time. They searched all around the yard and even walked up and down the street. But there was no sign of Ginger anywhere. It began to grow dark.

Amy fought back the tears as she and Ms. Somers walked slowly back toward the house. "We're never going to find him." She sighed. Then she stopped and listened hard.

"What is it, dear?" Ms. Somers asked.

Amy whispered, "I think I can hear him calling."

They stood still and listened. Sure enough, there was a distant meowing sound. Where was it coming from?

Slowly, they crept toward the sound. They didn't want to scare Ginger. The sound led them to the garden shed.

"He's in there!" cried Amy, rushing to the shed door. She pulled on the door handle. But it was locked! "Ginger, are you in there?" she called.

"You've taken a long time to find me," Ginger meowed crossly. "I'm fed up with being in here."

"I'll go and get the key," said Ms. Somers.

Amy talked to Ginger while they waited. "You poor thing," she said. "Did you follow Mr. Bradman in there when he was putting the tools away? I bet you did."

"Yes," meowed Ginger, "but he didn't see me and he locked me in!"

Ms. Somers seemed to take ages, but eventually she arrived and unlocked the door.

Ginger sprang up into Amy's arms. "At last! I'm upset!" he meowed.

While Ms. Somers relocked the shed, Amy hurried indoors up to her own apartment to give Ginger a drink of water.

"You'll have to stop being so curious," she said to him.

Ginger continued drinking. Being shut in the shed for so long had made him very thirsty. But he soon began to feel better and forgot what had happened. So, while Amy went to the bathroom to get ready for bed, he went to explore again.

First he noticed a closet door had been left ajar. "This looks promising," he meowed excitedly. He managed to pull it open wider with his paw, then crept inside. It was full of

brushes and brooms, mops and tools. Ginger had a great time sniffing around.

Then he saw the strange-looking machine that made lots of noise when Amy's mom was cleaning the apartment. Ginger didn't like the machine. It frightened him, and he hid behind the furniture when Amy's mom was pushing it around. He backed out of the closet in case he woke the machine up and went to find Amy.

Amy's schoolbag was on the floor in her bedroom. Amy was still in the bathroom. Ginger could hear her brushing her teeth.

"What's that delicious smell?" Ginger meowed as he poked his nose into the bag. "Cheese crackers!" he purred. "I love those!"

His face emerged from the bag a few moments later, covered in crumbs. He licked his paws and rubbed all over his face and whiskers until he was clean. Then he yawned. He was tired now.

When Amy came out of the bathroom, she

looked for Ginger. "I want to say good night to him," she said.

"All right," said Ms. Somers, "but be quick. Look at the time!"

But Ginger was nowhere to be found. Amy wasn't worried this time. She knew he was somewhere inside the apartment and, since she was very tired, she climbed into bed. Ms. Somers bent down and gave her a kiss.

"Give Ginger a hug for me when you find him," said Amy as she pushed her feet down under the quilt. "Aahh!" she screamed, pulling her knees up under her chin. "There's something in my bed! It's a big, hairy monster! Please get it out, Ms. Somers!"

Ms. Somers lifted the quilt and peered underneath. She started to chuckle. "Oh, dear," she said. "It is big. And it's hairy!"

"What is it?" Amy's blue eyes opened wide.

"I see two large, round amber eyes," said Ms. Somers.

"Get it out," said Amy again. "Please!"

Ms. Somers put her hand under the quilt and lifted out . . .

"Ginger!" squealed Amy.

"He must have been exploring under there and fallen asleep," said Ms. Somers. "He's had a tiring day! So have you. Sleep tight."

She put out the light, then carried Ginger out of Amy's room and closed the door.

The next morning, Amy didn't wake until her mom came into the room. She looked at her clock, then sat straight up. It was nine o'clock.

"Mom!" she cried. "Why didn't you wake me? I'll be late for school."

"It's Saturday, silly," laughed her mom. "And I thought you needed to sleep. Ms. Somers told me all about Ginger's antics when I got in last night!"

"Where is he?" asked Amy.

"He's had his breakfast and gone out in the yard already," said Amy's mom.

Amy climbed out of bed and ran to the

window. She could see Ginger's bright coat among the bushes. She tapped on the window and then opened it. Ginger looked up.

"I'm coming out after breakfast," Amy called.

"No hurry! I'm having a great time!" meowed Ginger, creeping forward, deeper into the undergrowth. He'd heard rustling noises somewhere in there. He thought it might be a bird. He loved trying to catch birds, but he didn't mind what this was as long as he could pounce on it.

When Amy came to find him, he was still stalking the mysterious creature that was making the leaves rustle.

"What are you doing?" Amy asked.

"I'm hunting," meowed Ginger.

"You look like a lion cub hunting in Africa," said Amy. "What is it?"

"I'm not sure yet," meowed Ginger.

Amy pushed her way into the bushes and peered through the thick mass of branches. A hedgehog scuttled out from the undergrowth and began to run on its little legs across the grass.

"There it goes!" Amy said.

Ginger dashed after the hedgehog, caught up with it, and got ready to pounce. The hedgehog stopped in its tracks and curled up in a spiky-looking ball. Ginger stopped and looked at the spiky ball in surprise.

Curiously, he reached out his paw to pat the ball, then jumped away, his back arched. "Ow!" he hissed. "That hurt!"

The hedgehog didn't move. "I don't want to play with you, either," Ginger meowed in disgust, then he ran off to explore something new.

Now the coast was clear, and the hedgehog ambled away again.

Amy laughed and went over to the yard swing. It was a lovely tall swing with a metal frame. She could go very high. Amy had been given it for her birthday a few months earlier.

She sat down on the seat and began working her way backward and forward. She had not been swinging for long when she saw Ginger loping toward her. She dragged her feet along the ground and came to a stop.

Ginger came up to her and nuzzled against her legs.

"Didn't you like that prickly old hedgehog?" she asked.

"No!" meowed Ginger, and he jumped up onto her lap.

"Do you want to swing?" asked Amy as she began again, pumping her legs to make the swing move.

As they went higher, Ginger wasn't sure he liked it.

"Help!" he yowled, crouching low and gripping Amy's sweatshirt with his claws. "I don't like this after all. Let me get down."

Amy stopped the swing as quickly as she could, and Ginger leaped from her lap onto the ground, landing safely in the grass. He dashed across the yard, pouncing on daisies and fallen twigs as he went. Avoiding the spot where the hedgehog had been, Ginger ran to the shed. On the roof a couple of birds twittered. Ginger looked up at them. He sat down and stared at them.

"You won't be able to get up there," called Amy, guessing Ginger's plan.

Oh, yes I will, Ginger thought. *No climb is too difficult for me.*

He crouched low, then sprang up onto the garden fence. The birds twittered in fright and flew off. He was disappointed to see them go, but quite pleased that he had scared them. One more leap! He heard Amy gasp as he landed on the shed roof. He felt so proud of himself that he sat down for a rest to celebrate.

"But I bet you won't be able to get down," called Amy. *Oh, yes I will!* Ginger thought again. But he wasn't ready to show Amy that new skill yet.

Ginger watched Amy going higher and

higher on the swing, then he yawned. It was time for a little nap. He stretched and lay down on his side on the warm shed roof in the sunshine and dozed.

He was woken by Amy's mom, calling Amy in for lunch. It seemed a long time since his breakfast, so it must be *his* lunchtime, too. He stood up and looked at the long drop down to the ground.

Amy jumped off the swing and ran over to the shed. "So you're stuck up there, aren't you?" she asked.

"Of course not," meowed Ginger, although it was the highest he had ever been and he wasn't feeling very brave.

"Should I get the stepladder and help you down?" asked Amy.

That helped Ginger make up his mind. He moved to the edge of the shed roof. "Look out!" he meowed. "I'm coming down!"

Amy stepped back as Ginger leaped off the shed. He dropped gracefully down to the concrete path below. Amazed at his success, he then ran madly around and around the yard.

"Did you see that?" he meowed loudly to Amy and her mom and anyone else who was listening. "I could get down from anywhere! Anywhere at all!"

3

A few days later, when Amy walked out of school, she found Ms. Somers waiting for her by the gate. Her mom was on the day shift, which meant she wouldn't be home until later in the evening.

Amy ran ahead of Ms. Somers, in a hurry to get home to see Ginger. He was sitting on the doorstep when Amy arrived and he trotted down the path to meet her. He butted Amy's legs with his head, and she bent to scratch the side of his face.

"Have you been a good kitten today?" she asked.

Ginger pretended he hadn't heard. "I'm ready for my dinner," he meowed.

"I think he's hungry," Amy said to Ms. Somers, who was unlocking the front door.

"He's always hungry," laughed Ms. Somers. "You feed him while I make a snack."

Amy gave Ginger his food, then went out into the yard.

"Do you want to eat outside?' Ms. Somers called from her kitchen.

"Yes, please," Amy called back from the swing.

Amy's mom didn't like her feeding Ginger from the table, but since they were having a picnic, Ms. Somers said she could, just this once. Even though Ginger ate every scrap of his food, he still had a little room to help Amy eat hers.

Ginger liked everything. First he had some of an egg-salad sandwich, then a piece of sausage, then crackers, then a nibble of cheese. Now he was really full! He snoozed for a few minutes, then shot off on his usual run around the yard, chasing his tail and rolling in the grass.

"This is more fun than going to the theater!" laughed Ms. Somers.

Ginger loved having an audience. When he had finished his antics, he decided to demonstrate his new trick of climbing on the shed roof.

"Oh, my!" gasped Ms. Somers when she saw what he was doing. "He'll get stuck."

"Don't worry," said Amy. "He got down easily enough last time."

Ginger was safely on the roof by now. "Look at me!" he meowed. "Don't you think I'm smart?"

Amy laughed. "He'll be all right," she said. "He could probably get down from anywhere!"

Amy helped Ms. Somers clear the table and take the dishes inside. After they had washed the dishes, they called Ginger to come in.

But he didn't appear.

"Oh, no!" sighed Amy. "Not again!"

"Perhaps he's still on the shed roof," said Ms. Somers. But when Amy ran over to the shed, there was no sign of him. She wasn't really worried, though. Last time she thought he was lost, he had turned up in the end. She walked back to the house.

Amy and Ms. Somers searched in all the usual places, and they stopped and listened every so often in case he was calling. But they heard nothing.

"I hope he isn't really lost!" Amy said worriedly. "I wish Mom was here to help us find him."

She looked around again. Then, suddenly, she noticed something tiny and orange on the roof of the house. *It isn't. It can't be!* Amy couldn't believe it. But it was!

"Ginger! How did you get up there?" she yelled.

Ms. Somers rushed over to Amy and looked up. "Oh, my goodness!" she said.

Amy and Ms. Somers hurried closer to the house to get a better look.

"Oh!" said Amy, biting her lip nervously. "His little mouth's opening and closing. He's calling us, but we can't hear him from way up there. I bet he wants us to get him down."

"Oh, dear, yes," Ms. Somers said anxiously as Amy tried to decide what to do.

She ran to the back of the house where an old wooden ladder lay on the ground. For many years it had been used for leaning up against the trees when the apples were ready to be picked in Ms. Somers's garden. She bent to pick it up.

"No, Amy!" called Ms. Somers. "Don't even think of it. That's much too dangerous."

"But he might fall!" cried Amy, chewing her fingernails. "What are we going to do?"

"Go indoors and see if you can coax him down," said Ms. Somers.

Amy ran into the house. She raced up to her bedroom, flung open the window, and leaned out, craning her neck to see Ginger. "Where are you, boy?" she called.

Amy heard a sorrowful meow above and farther along the roof, but she couldn't see the kitten.

"I'm in my bedroom, Ginger," she called. "Can you come down to me?"

"No!" meowed Ginger pitifully.

Amy tried calling him a few more times, but he just meowed back and didn't seem to want to move. She ran back down to the garden to find Ms. Somers.

"I couldn't even see him," she said. "There's no way I could reach him, and he seems too scared to come down."

"In that case," said Ms. Somers, "we'd better call the Fire Department."

*   *   *

37

Ginger had felt so brave when he'd climbed from the roof of the garden shed, onto the fence post, then up the gutter. And when he'd reached the top of the roof, he'd felt like the king of the world!

Well done! he had meowed to himself as he heaved himself up the last roof shingle and sat, out of breath, looking down at the garden. *I just had to see what it was like up here and I knew I could climb anywhere!*

But he soon realized what a long way down it was, and he wasn't at all sure he could get down the way he had come up!

Amy and Ms. Somers had gone indoors, so he was all alone. "Help! I can't get down," he meowed.

He could see far, into the next yard where the fierce dog had been. And along the street where Amy went to school every day. But although he could see plenty of people, none of them noticed him.

Ginger began to feel very sorry for himself.

"Help!" he meowed again. "Will someone please get me down?"

But nobody heard him. *What if I have to stay up here forever?* Ginger thought sadly.

Suddenly, he saw Amy come running out into the yard again. He could faintly hear her. She was calling him.

"Help!" he meowed with all his heart. "Amy! Here I am! Up here!"

He stood up and balanced along the peak of the roof, calling as loudly as he could. "Please look up," he meowed. "Amy, I'm here!"

At last, Amy noticed Ginger. He could just hear her shouting and see her pointing up at him. He saw Ms. Somers come and stand beside her, then Amy ran into the house. A moment later, Ginger could clearly hear her calling him, but he couldn't see her. She was in her bedroom, asking him if he could get to her.

But Ginger was too frightened to go anywhere. Amy stopped calling and soon he saw her back in the yard with Ms. Somers. *What now?* he thought desperately. But soon, Amy was back in her room, talking to him again. Ginger leaned forward so he could hear her.

"We're calling the Fire Department," Amy shouted. "Don't worry. You're going to be all right."

Ginger didn't know what the Fire Department was, but he hoped it was going to help him down. "Hurry up," he meowed. "I'm frightened to be by myself."

"They won't be long," Amy called.

"Good!" meowed Ginger.

Suddenly, a bright red noisy machine, much, much bigger and noisier than the machine Amy's mom used to clean the house, came zooming around the corner of the next street. Ginger almost slipped down the gray roof shingles in fright and only just managed to hold on with his claws. This machine was a hundred times more frightening than the machine in the broom closet. Ginger's heart pounded loudly in his chest. He didn't know what had terrified him more, the noisy red machine or fear of falling off the roof.

The enormous noisy machine stopped on the street outside the house. Then it became quiet and Ginger could hear Amy's voice again.

"They're here," she shouted. "It's the Fire Department."

So that's the Fire Department, Ginger thought, *but how is this frightening monster going to help me?*

Several people dressed strangely, with big hard-looking helmets, climbed out of the machine. They lifted a long ladder from the top of it. Longer and longer it grew until it rested on the roof near Ginger. Ginger watched as one of the strangely dressed people climbed the ladder.

"I'm frightened," Ginger meowed down to Amy. "I'm scared of being stuck up here and

I'm scared of that noisy red machine and now I'm scared of that person climbing up the ladder."

"It's all right," Amy called from her bedroom. "Just let the firefighter bring you down. I'll see you in the yard."

A group of people had gathered on the path outside the gate. They were shouting and pointing. Ginger thought he could see Tom, Mr. Bradman's son, with some of his friends.

The firefighter was climbing higher and higher and had almost reached Ginger. Ginger thought the person looked very strange. Nervously, Ginger crawled backward along the roof, away from the firefighter's outstretched hands. But then he spotted Amy down in the yard, and he remembered what she had told him. He knew he had to let the firefighter carry him down, so he crept forward again.

Ginger didn't like the dark clothes or the large helmet that hid the firefighter's face. But he closed his eyes, then felt himself being lifted off the roof and pushed inside the fire-fighter's dark jacket. Slowly, the firefighter began to climb down the ladder. "You're going to be all right, Ginger."

Where have I heard that voice before? Ginger thought. It made him feel much better.

By the time they had reached the bottom of the ladder, he was beginning to purr. And there was Amy, waiting for him. She held out her arms and the firefighter handed him over.

"Thanks," said Amy, all smiles now that Ginger was safe. "Say 'thank you' to the firefighter, Ginger."

Ginger turned to look at the person who had just rescued him. The firefighter took off the large helmet, and a very familiar face emerged. Ginger meowed in surprise. It was Amy's mom!

So that's what she does when she goes off each day!

"Thank you," purred Ginger as he snuggled into Amy's arms. He looked up at Amy.

She was grinning at her mom. "Thanks, Mom," said Amy. "I was hoping it would be you!"

"I wouldn't have let anyone else rescue our Ginger," laughed her mom. "But perhaps he'll learn not to be quite so adventurous in the future."

"I don't know about that," purred Ginger. "But I'll try!"

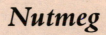

Nutmeg

1

Nutmeg pushed her nose against the door. It moved slightly. She pushed again, harder this time, and the door slowly swung open. *Should I go in?* she wondered. Nutmeg had never been inside this room before without her owner, Dan Brown — or his sister, Helen, or their mom and dad. But for some reason someone had left the door slightly open today.

There must be so many new places to explore and

things to play with in there. It won't do any harm. I'll go in, just for a quick look, Nutmeg thought. Keeping her eyes and ears alert, she sneaked into the room.

"Who's a pretty boy?" The squawk was so loud that it made Nutmeg's ears hurt and her heart patter inside her. She scuttled under a low table. She had forgotten Sailor!

Sailor was a very old, very large parrot that had belonged to Mrs. Brown since before nine-year-old Dan or his older sister, Helen, were born. Sailor was allowed outside his cage during the daytime. He had to stay in this room, but it was large and airy so Sailor had plenty of space to fly around. Throughout the day, Sailor's cage sat empty at the side of the room, but its door was always left open. As regular as clockwork, the parrot made his way into the cage each evening. Sailor liked to feel safe at night while he slept. He liked the door of his cage to be closed, and a thick cloth thrown over it.

"Who's a pretty boy?" Sailor asked again.

Nutmeg peeped out from the safety of her hiding place. She was not sure whether she should be frightened of him or not. He was so big! "I'm a girl, actually," she meowed.

Sailor was perched on the back of a chair near his cage. He flapped his enormous wings and showed off the beautiful colors of his feathers — blue, red, green, and yellow. Then he preened himself with his long, hooked beak, not taking his beady eyes off Nutmeg for a second. "Who's a pretty boy?" he squawked again.

Nutmeg thought he was teasing her. "I know my fur isn't as bright as your feathers," she meowed, "but I'm proud of my golden-brown coat."

Sailor just sat and stared at Nutmeg. She began to feel braver. *Never mind that nuisance of a parrot. I've come in here to explore,* she decided. She turned her back on Sailor and scampered across the room.

First she found a rather interesting wire. It

trailed along the floor by the television. Holding it between her paws, Nutmeg rolled over and over, getting herself thoroughly tangled up. She lay still for a moment, then wriggled her way out.

Looking around for the next game, she saw Sailor glaring at her with his little black eyes. He had followed her across the room.

"Hello, Sailor!" he squawked.

Nutmeg tried to ignore him. She lay on her side on the thick fireplace rug and began to wash herself the way Bracken, her mother, had taught her. She licked her front paws and used them all over her face and ears, then she lifted her legs one by one. Finally, she washed her cream tummy and throat. That was better! If only that parrot didn't make so much noise!

"Hello, Sailor!" Sailor squawked. "Hello, Sailor!"

Nutmeg's tail began to thump a slow, steady beat on the carpet. Sailor was making her cross.

"Hello, Sailor!" Sailor squawked with an ear-piercing sound. "Hello, Sailor!"

"Silly old Sailor!" hissed Nutmeg. With one swift movement she rolled over onto her feet and sprang at the parrot.

Sailor flapped his wings noisily and flew to the top of his empty cage, where he sat screeching at full volume. "Get off! Get off! Get off!" he cried out at the top of his voice. There were thundering footsteps as Dan dashed into the room, followed by his mom.

Sailor stopped squawking and put his head to one side.

Mrs. Brown looked at Sailor, balanced on the cage, his wings still beating and his feathers sticking out at all angles. Then she looked at Nutmeg. "Don't be naughty, Nutmeg!" she said. "What are you doing in here?"

"Just playing," meowed Nutmeg.

"How did she get in here?" Mrs. Brown asked Dan.

"I don't know," Dan replied.

"You know what we agreed when we first got her," said Mrs. Brown sternly. "That we'd keep those two apart when none of us was in the room to watch them."

Dan picked up his kitten. "I can't believe a tiny thing like you managed to ruffle Sailor's feathers," he whispered, smiling.

Nutmeg climbed onto his shoulder, right next to his ear. She liked it up there. She could snuggle into the top of his sweater.

"What did you do to poor old Sailor?" Dan asked, stroking her fur all the way down her back to the tip of her soft tail.

"I was only trying to catch him," Nutmeg purred, trying to look cute.

"She's a sweet little thing," said Mrs. Brown, "but so naughty!"

"She is only three months old," said Dan. "Kittens are supposed to be mischievous at that age."

Sailor flew across the room and perched on the television. "Who's a pretty boy?" he squawked.

"You are, of course," said Mrs. Brown, feeling in her pocket for a peanut.

Sailor took the nut in his claw and broke open the shell with his beak. "You're nuts!" he squawked. "You're nuts!"

Dan laughed. Sailor was always picking up new sayings. "Come on, Nutmeg," he said. "Let's go to my room."

He walked across the wide hall with Nutmeg balanced on his shoulder, up the stairs and into his bedroom. "It's a little quieter in here," he said.

He put Nutmeg down on the floor, then picked up a sock and waved it in front of her. She pounced, but Dan pulled it away just in time. Then he trailed it across the floor for the kitten to chase. It was fun.

Some time later, Dan left Nutmeg chasing the little ball from his football game while he played on his computer.

"I think I'll explore some more!" meowed Nutmeg, and she climbed up into an open drawer and turned around and around, mixing up all the clothes.

"Don't be naughty, Nutmeg!" sighed Dan. "Mom will be annoyed if she sees what you've done!"

"Sorry!" meowed Nutmeg. She jumped down and went over to Dan, leaping onto his lap.

Climbing onto his desk, Nutmeg walked across Dan's computer keyboard.

"Oh, Nutmeg! Now look what you've done," said Dan as the game he was playing came to a sudden end. But he wasn't really mad. How could he be upset with such a cute little thing? He lifted Nutmeg gently down onto the floor and began another game.

A few minutes later, Dan realized that Nutmeg had become very quiet. *What's she up to now?* he wondered. Then he heard a scratching sound and a faint meow. It didn't take him long to find her. She had crawled into one of the tunnels from his remote-control racecar track and was stuck!

"Nutmeg!" he laughed as he gently pulled her free. "You're the nosiest cat in the world!"

"I know!" meowed Nutmeg.

Dan watched Nutmeg as she continued playing. He was really glad he had chosen her out of Bracken's litter of nine very different kittens. Well, she had chosen him, really. . . .

Dan's family had heard about the kittens from Mr. Bradman, who was changing the layout of their large yard. He had invited them to his house to see the litter when they were about four weeks old. Dan hadn't noticed Nutmeg at first. But when he had picked up his coat to get a tissue, he'd found her asleep, in one of his sleeves! She'd crawled in when no one was looking and curled up for a nap.

Three weeks later, when Dan and Mrs. Brown had gone back to the Bradmans' to get Nutmeg, she had scampered toward them, as if she remembered them. And she had settled quickly into her new home.

Dan went back to his computer game and Nutmeg looked around for more places to explore. She spotted that the bedroom door wasn't completely shut. She bounded over to it, pushed her tiny paw into the crack, and pulled. It opened farther.

She looked back at Dan. He was concentrating hard on his computer, and didn't notice Nutmeg squeezing out of the room.

"What a smart kitten I am!" she meowed as she ran out onto the landing. She really was getting very good at opening doors. She poked her head through the rungs of the banister at the top of the stairs and looked down into the hall.

It was a very big house and although she had been with the Browns for quite a while now, there were still a few rooms that she hadn't had a chance to explore. Today, she could see that the kitchen door was wide open. She would go in there first.

One step at a time, she bounced down the stairs, then she galloped across the hall and into the kitchen. Nobody was there. "Good!" she meowed quietly. "I can go where I please and do what I want."

Nutmeg decided to explore some of the kitchen shelves first. Softly, she jumped up and began to prowl along one of the lower ones, smelling each box or bag that she came to.

Everything had a different scent. And some things smelled delicious!

Nutmeg's mouth watered. She reached out her paw and tried to open a few of them, but had no luck, though a few dropped off the shelf and onto the floor.

Then she came to a big blue-and-white-striped bag. It was open at the top, but she was too small to see what was in it, so she stood on her hind paws and stretched up, leaning against the bag, trying to see inside.

Suddenly, the bag began to tip and then it toppled over. Loads of powdery white stuff fell out all over the shelf. And all over Nutmeg. Some fell onto the floor and white clouds of it filled the air.

"Aaa . . . tchoo!" sneezed Nutmeg as it went up her nose. "Aaa . . . tchoo!"

"There's someone in the kitchen!" she

heard Helen call as more and more white stuff got up her nose and made it feel ticklish again.

"Aaa . . . tchoo!" Nutmeg sneezed more flour into the air as Mrs. Brown and Helen came into the kitchen. Helen laughed when she saw Nutmeg, but Mrs. Brown didn't.

"Oh, Nutmeg — you're so naughty!" cried Mrs. Brown.

"I didn't know we had a white kitten," said Helen, picking up Nutmeg. "Look at the condition you're in!"

"I was only having a look around," meowed Nutmeg.

Helen put the kitten on a towel on the kitchen table and began to brush the flour from her fur. Nutmeg wriggled around, trying to escape. Then she caught sight of a bright flash of color. Sailor was watching from the doorway. But not for long. Mrs. Brown quickly went and lifted him up, his claws curling around her hand. "How did this parrot get

out of the living room?" she asked as she carried him away.

"He seems to be following me around,"
meowed Nutmeg. "He always turns up when
I'm having the most fun. *And* when I'm being
yelled at!"

2

Mrs. Brown came back and began to sweep up the mess. Nutmeg shook herself and sneezed again. Almost all of the flour had gone now, and Helen let Nutmeg jump down from the kitchen table. She scampered out into the hall in case Helen changed her mind. And there in front of her, the door to Sailor's room was still open!

"You're nuts!" Nutmeg heard as she crept into the room. "You're nuts!"

Nutmeg took no notice of Sailor. She jumped onto the windowsill to see what was happening outside. But as she landed, her paws skidded and she knocked over a vase. The vase wobbled, sloshing out water that trickled across the windowsill and dripped down onto the carpet. Nutmeg froze, wondering if the vase was going to topple over onto the floor and break. She'd already been in enough trouble for one day.

"You're nuts!" Sailor screeched.

"Be quiet!" Nutmeg hissed back, still watching the vase. But it seemed to have settled and was still again. Phew!

Nutmeg looked at the water on the carpet. There was a dark stain down the wallpaper below the windowsill, too. She hoped Mrs. Brown wouldn't be too mad.

"I'd better get away from here," she meowed

to herself, "before anyone sees what I've done."

"Hello, Sailor!" the parrot squawked as Nutmeg ran across the room toward the door.

Nutmeg ignored Sailor. *He really was silly*, she thought. But as she passed by the table, Nutmeg couldn't resist jumping up to see if there was anything interesting up there.

Sure enough, she found masses of bright, strange-shaped pieces. She'd seen these before. Helen had called it a jigsaw puzzle. The pieces seemed to Nutmeg to be asking to be pushed around. She liked the way they skidded across the shiny surface of the polished wood.

Just when she was becoming really skilled at hitting the pieces a long way, the door opened and Helen came in. "Nutmeg!" she cried, making a deep frown across her forehead. "I'd spent ages on that — and now it's ruined!"

"What's the matter?" Mrs. Brown called from the kitchen.

"Come and see what Nutmeg's done now!" cried Helen. "I'll have to put it together all over again!"

Nutmeg gulped. She could see that Helen was upset. "I didn't know," she meowed. "I thought anyone could play with your game."

Mrs. Brown rushed into the room. "Don't be naughty, Nutmeg!" she said loudly when she saw Helen's puzzle.

Nutmeg hung her head. She didn't mean to upset anybody, but she wasn't having a very good day.

"You're nuts!" squawked Sailor, but this time nobody laughed.

Nutmeg leaped at him, but he flew to the safety of the top of his cage again. "Get off! Get off!" he squawked.

"Don't be naughty, Nutmeg!" Mrs. Brown repeated. Then she noticed the wet patch under the window.

"Was this you, Nutmeg?" she sighed, looking for something to mop up the water. "What are we going to do with you?"

"I don't know," meowed Nutmeg. "But I'll try and be good from now on."

The family had fish and chips for lunch that day. Nutmeg could smell the delicious fish as soon as Mrs. Brown and the children arrived home and unwrapped it in the kitchen. Nutmeg even jumped on the table to get a better look at it. But Mrs. Brown lifted her down. "None for you," she said.

Dan picked Nutmeg up. "I'll give you some of mine," he whispered in her ear. Everyone sat around the dining table to eat. Nutmeg sat under the table, hoping for some scraps to fall her way, but she was disappointed.

"You have to wait until we've finished," whispered Dan.

Sailor watched from a distance. He had been fed already.

"What's for dinner?" he squawked. "What's for dinner?"

"Fish and chips," said Dan. "Hey, should I teach him to say it?"

"Why not?" said Mrs. Brown. "He likes learning new words."

Dan finished eating, then he took his plate into the kitchen to put the leftover fish into Nutmeg's dish. Nutmeg sniffed the little white pieces of fish. She had never tasted it before, but her mouth watered and she knew she was going to love it. She nibbled the fish and licked the plate until it was clean. While she ate, she could hear Dan talking to Sailor.

"Fish and chips, Sailor," he said. "Come on, say it — fish and chips. Fish and chips. It's easy — fish and chips."

Nutmeg came back in from the kitchen to watch.

Sailor took a deep breath and closed one eye. Then he lifted his head and opened his beak. "Chish and fips!" he squawked. "Chish and fips!"

"No, you silly!" laughed Dan. "Fish and chips!"

But Sailor seemed to prefer what he had first said. "Silly Sailor!" he squawked. "Chish and fips! Chish and fips!"

Everyone was laughing at Sailor, but Nutmeg felt full and rather sleepy. Nobody noticed her creep over and jump up onto the windowsill again. She was more careful this time, and didn't knock the vase over. She made herself comfortable and fell fast asleep in the sunshine.

Nutmeg woke with a start. She sat up, her heart racing and her bright eyes wide with fright. What had woken her up?

She soon found out: Sailor!

"Chish and fips!" he was squawking. "Chish and fips!"

Mr. Brown was home from work and Dan was getting Sailor to show off his new phrase. Mr. Brown was roaring with laughter.

"Well done, Sailor," he chuckled. "You're brilliant! And well done, Dan, for teaching him."

"What's for dinner?" squawked Sailor very loudly. "Chish and fips!"

Nutmeg had had enough of the parrot's loud voice. She yawned, stood up on the windowsill, stretching her back into a high arch, then she jumped nimbly down onto the floor and darted from the room. She crept across the hall and up the stairs, wondering if Helen was in her room. She would go and see.

Helen was sitting at her dressing table painting her nails with glittery polish. She was going out to a school dance later that evening. She saw Nutmeg in the mirror as soon as the kitten entered the room. "Hello, mischief," she said. "Thought you'd come and disturb me, did you?"

"There's lots in here I haven't discovered yet," meowed Nutmeg.

"I hope you're not going to break anything," said Helen.

"I'll try not to," Nutmeg replied.

Suddenly, a bell rang, making Nutmeg jump. It was that thing in the hall that they called the phone. The ringing stopped and Nutmeg heard Mr. Brown's voice.

"Helen," Mr. Brown shouted. "Phone!"

"Okay, Dad," called Helen as she leaped up from her dressing table and ran downstairs.

Nutmeg immediately rushed over to the dressing table. She wanted to know what Helen was putting on her fingernails. It was very sparkly. Then something else caught her eye. Helen's hair band was just waiting to be pounced on. But as she pounced, Nutmeg knocked over Helen's sparkly stuff.

She looked at the shiny pool that was growing on the dressing table. "Uh-oh . . ." she meowed, alarmed. She reached out her paw and touched the edge of it. It felt very sticky. Nutmeg sniffed at it, then quickly pulled her nose away. It smelled horrible! It made her feel sick.

Quickly she leaped down, away from the smell. She tried to shake the stuff from her paw, but it had stuck fast.

The closet was open. Nutmeg decided she would explore in there until she felt better.

It was very dark inside the closet, but Nutmeg could see clearly. There was one of Helen's sneakers in the corner, so she jumped into it. She fit very well, but she soon grew bored with sitting still, so she jumped out again. She chewed on a shoelace for a while, then pulled at a belt that was hanging from one of Helen's skirts.

Suddenly, Nutmeg froze in terror. Two hollow black eyes were staring at her from a shiny white face. There were red circles on the cheeks and the laughing mouth looked big enough to swallow Nutmeg.

"Help!" she meowed timidly. But nobody came to rescue her from this frightening creature. "Stay away!" she hissed.

But the face seemed to loom bigger and bigger. Nutmeg backed away into the far corner of the closet. "Help!" she meowed again. But still nobody came. She would have to stay with this terrifying creature forever.

At that moment, Nutmeg heard Helen come back into the room.

"Oh, no!" Helen said. Her voice sounded angry. She must have found the spilled, smelly, sticky stuff. "Where's that naughty kitten? Nutmeg! Nutmeg! Where are you?"

"I'm in here," Nutmeg tried to meow. But being frightened made her voice very weak. Now she didn't know which was worse, being yelled at by Helen or being trapped with the frightening creature.

She decided the face was much worse. Helen was sure to forgive her. "I'm here," she meowed louder.

"I can hear you," called Helen. "But I can't see you."

Nutmeg couldn't stand the face any longer. She knew she had to be brave and walk past it. "Stay away!" she hissed again as she backed slowly toward the closet door. "Ugly thing, I don't like you," she hissed. Nutmeg was shaking so much she began to fall over her own paws, but at last she reached the closet door and dashed out, still trembling all over.

Dan was standing in the doorway of Helen's room. He had been in his own room and had heard his sister call out. He looked at Helen, then Nutmeg, then at the pool of sticky nail polish.

"Don't be naughty, Nutmeg!" he said, but then he noticed her enormous wide eyes and realized that she was shaking. "She's frightened," he said, looking angrily at his sister. "What have you done to her?"

"Nothing!" shouted Helen. "I came back from the phone and found this! I assumed Nutmeg had done it. That's all. I didn't know she'd gone into the closet."

Dan went over to Nutmeg and picked her up. He held her close and snuggled her into the neck of his sweater. "Poor little thing," he said. "She's shaking like a leaf." He stroked Nutmeg gently. "What's the matter?" he asked her.

Nutmeg looked at the closet. "T-there's s-something t-terrible in t-there," Nutmeg meowed.

3

"I've never seen her like this before," said Dan. "Something in the closet must have scared her."

"In the closet?" said Helen doubtfully. She opened the closet door wide and peered in. Then she began to laugh. She bent down and pulled something out.

It was the horrible face! Nutmeg disappeared down inside Dan's sweater.

"It's all right, Nutmeg," said Dan, lifting her out. "Look! It's only a silly old mask that Helen wore to a costume party last week."

Nutmeg looked. Although she still didn't like how it looked, the face wasn't as fierce out in the light, cheerful bedroom. And she trusted Dan and believed what he said. Gradually, she stopped shaking. As Helen and Dan stroked her, Nutmeg began to purr.

"Hello, Sailor!" came the sudden squawk from Helen's doorway. Dan and Helen jumped almost as much as Nutmeg did. "What's for dinner? Chish and fips! Who's a pretty boy?"

"Have you escaped from the living room again?" Helen asked the parrot.

"Who's a pretty boy?" squawked Sailor. "Give us a kiss!"

"Not likely!" laughed Helen. "Anyway, how long have you been there, watching?"

"Clever boy!" squawked Sailor. "Chish and fips! Chish and fips!"

Nutmeg had heard enough. She leaped out of Dan's arms at Sailor. This time he only just managed to fly out of her reach onto the landing. He sat perched on the banister rail, complaining loudly. "Get off! Get off! Get off!" he squawked.

"Is Nutmeg being naughty?" Mrs. Brown shouted loudly from downstairs. She sounded cross. "And who let Sailor out of the living room?"

Dan and Helen leaned over the banister.

"We didn't," said Dan. "We were both up here all the time."

"This is getting ridiculous," said Mrs. Brown. "We all know he shouldn't be out of there."

"I think he lets himself out," said Dan.

"Don't be silly," said Mr. Brown, who had joined his wife in the hall. "A parrot couldn't do that."

"I bet Sailor could!" said Helen. "He's smart enough!"

"And, Dan, you'll have to find a way to stop that kitten of yours from bothering Sailor," said Mrs. Brown.

Dan and Helen laughed. Dan held Nutmeg up next to Sailor.

"Look at the difference in size," said Dan.

"As if a tiny animal like that could do much harm to a great big bird like Sailor!" said Helen.

Nutmeg purred. "It won't stop me from trying to catch him, though. I just love to see his bright feathers ruffled!"

The following day, Dan was getting dressed. He was grinning to himself as he pulled on his sweatshirt. He was thinking about all the mischief Nutmeg had been up to. He tied the laces of his sneakers and headed out of his bedroom. Just then, he heard a shout.

"Don't be naughty, Nutmeg!" his mom was screeching.

What on earth has Nutmeg done now? Dan

thought. *It must be something really terrible for Mom to make such a fuss!*

Dan leaped down the stairs two at a time. As he reached the bottom step, he glanced into the kitchen. And there, through the kitchen window, he could see his mom! She was in the yard hanging the wash out on the line and talking to Mr. Bradman.

Mom moved quickly, Dan thought. *And she looks quite calm already.* He dashed through the kitchen and out into the yard.

"Hello, Dan," said Mr. Bradman. "How's that young kitten doing? Still as inquisitive as ever?"

"Yes. Well, actually, that's why I came out," said Dan. "I heard Mom shout and I wondered what Nutmeg had done."

"Me?" said Mrs. Brown. "Shout?"

"Yes," said Dan.

"When?"

"Just now."

Mrs. Brown smiled and shook her head.

"Not me," she said. "I've been out here with Mr. Bradman for at least ten minutes, haven't I, Tim?"

Mr. Bradman nodded. "It's true," he said with a chuckle. "And not a single shout has passed her lips. You must have imagined it, Dan."

"No," said Dan, puzzled. "I definitely heard it."

"In fact, I haven't seen Nutmeg this morning," said Mrs. Brown. "I thought she must be upstairs with you or Helen."

Suddenly, they were all shocked to silence.

"Don't be naughty, Nutmeg!" they heard. "Ha! Ha! Ha! Ha!"

"I told you!" said Dan.

"It certainly sounds like me," said Mrs. Brown. "What's going on?"

They all ran indoors and met Helen and Mr. Brown in the hall.

"Mom!" said Helen. "What's Nutmeg done?"

Before Mrs. Brown could answer, they heard it again.

"Don't be naughty, Nutmeg! Ha! Ha! Ha! Ha!"

The sound was coming from the living room. Dan dashed in, followed by the rest of the family and Mr. Bradman.

What they saw made them all laugh. Sailor was cheerfully flapping around the room, screaming in a perfect imitation of Mrs. Brown's voice, "Don't be naughty, Nutmeg! Ha! Ha! Ha! Ha!"

But where was Nutmeg?

It was Dan who spotted her. She was huddled in the bottom of the huge parrot cage looking very sorry for herself. The cage door was firmly closed.

"Help!" Nutmeg meowed in a pitiful little voice. "Let me out. That bad old bird has locked me in."

"How did she get in there?" said Helen.

Dan looked at Sailor, who seemed very

pleased with himself. "It must have been Sailor," he said, opening the cage door and reaching in for Nutmeg. "He must have shut her in."

Helen laughed.

"Don't be silly, Dan," said Mr. Brown. "A parrot couldn't do something like that."

"Yes, he could," said Dan, placing Nutmeg on her favorite place on his shoulder. "All he had to do was wait until Nutmeg went to explore his cage. She's so nosy, she was bound to go in sometime, weren't you, Nutmeg?"

"Yes," admitted Nutmeg, meowing pitifully. "That clever old parrot tricked me!"

"I always knew my parrot was intelligent!" laughed Mrs. Brown.

"And I still bet he's the one who's been opening the living room door," said Dan.

"You're probably right," said his mom. "We could test him. Then we'll know what to expect from now on."

Everyone left the living room and Mrs. Brown closed the door firmly behind them. They waited silently in the hall. But not for long! There was a faint scratching sound as the handle on the outside of the door rattled and began to move. A few moments later, Sailor appeared in the doorway.

"Who's a clever boy?" he squawked.

"You are!" laughed Mrs. Brown. "More than we realized!"

Mr. Bradman went back outside to draw up plans for the yard. The Brown family went back in the living room and sat down.

"It seems we've been blaming Nutmeg for all the mischief around here," laughed Mrs. Brown. "But it looks as if Sailor can be just as naughty!"

"There isn't a reason to keep them apart any longer," said Mrs. Brown. "Sailor has certainly proved he can look after himself!"

Nutmeg purred her agreement about that!

She snuggled into the top of Dan's sweatshirt, warm and happy now. She loved being part of the Brown family.

"Perhaps you won't be quite so naughty from now on, Nutmeg," Dan whispered.

Nutmeg rubbed her face against his chin, then looked at Sailor with new respect.

"Or maybe Sailor and I will make mischief together!" she purred. "That would be fun!"

And, as Nutmeg watched, Sailor winked at her.

Clove

1

Clove scampered into the large kitchen in the Bradmans' house. She had been playing in the hall with two of her sisters, but she was tired now and ready for a snooze. She climbed onto the edge of the big cat basket in the corner of the room and jumped in beside Bracken, her mother.

Bracken stirred in her sleep and made room for the chubby little charcoal-colored kitten.

Clove snuggled up against her. She was eight weeks old now and no longer drinking her mother's milk, but she still loved the warmth of Bracken's thick tortoiseshell coat. Best of all, she loved to hear her mother's soft purring voice.

"You're such a quiet little thing," Bracken purred when Clove had settled herself comfortably. "Not as nosy or adventurous as some of your brothers and sisters, especially Ginger and Nutmeg."

"I've missed those two since they've gone to their new homes, but at least there's more room in the basket," Clove meowed back. "And it's much quieter!"

"It won't be long before you have a new home," said Bracken, cleaning behind Clove's ears with her rough tongue.

"But I like it here with you," meowed Clove. *The Bradmans' house, with you to look after me, is where I belong!* the little kitten said to herself.

"You all have to leave here sooner or later,"

purred Bracken. "The family couldn't possibly look after so many kittens forever."

But I'm really quiet and not much trouble, Clove thought. She didn't want to leave the Bradmans' house. It was all she knew.

"The Bradmans will find someone to love you," Bracken went on.

Tom and Ellie Bradman came into the kitchen. They walked over to the basket and looked down at Bracken and Clove.

"Isn't Clove sweet?" said Ellie, bending over the basket. "Just look at that fat tummy. Like a dark-gray fur ball!"

She reached down and tickled Clove's tummy. "Oh, yes, I like that!" Clove meowed, wriggling onto her back and sticking her paws in the air.

"Look!" laughed Ellie. "She loves that!"

"She's so good-natured and affectionate," said Tom. He gently scooped Clove up in his hands and then cradled her in his arms. "Listen to her purring," he said.

Maybe if I'm extra-cute they'll decide to keep me, Clove thought, purring as loudly as she could.

"Woof! Woof! Woof!" Lottie, the large golden retriever, rushed into the kitchen with one of Clove's sisters, Amber, right behind her. She bounded over to the sink and lifted her front paws up onto the counter so that she could look out of the kitchen window. Her tail started wagging as she saw what she was looking for.

"That must be Dad home from work," said Ellie, and she ran to open the back door.

"Woof! Woof! Woof!"

Clove hid in Tom's chest. "I do like Lottie," she meowed, "but she's just a little loud for me."

"Quiet, Lottie!" said Tom. "You're frightening Clove."

Mr. Bradman came up the sidewalk and stood in the doorway to take off his muddy boots. He came into the kitchen and smiled at Tom and Ellie.

"Hello. I've had a great day!" he said, bending to make a fuss over Lottie. "I'm working on a new orchard for old Mr. Miller."

"Oh, yes," said Ellie. "Janie told me she'd seen you in her grandpa's garden."

"How do you know Janie?" asked Mr. Bradman.

"She's in my class at school," said Ellie.

Mr. Bradman took off his coat and washed his hands. Then he noticed Clove in Tom's arms and he stroked her head. "So they haven't found a home for you yet?" he asked her.

"No," purred Clove. "But I don't mind."

"I'm a little worried," said Tom. "I know we still have several kittens to find homes for, but we must make sure we find the right place for Clove especially. She's a shy little thing and needs lots of love and attention."

"Didn't Mr. Miller once have a big old cat?" asked Ellie.

"Yes," said Mr. Bradman. "Old Monty — it

must be about a year since he died. Mmm, I wonder if Mr. Miller would like a kitten. I'll ask him tomorrow."

"Good idea," said Tom, putting Clove back in the basket beside Bracken. "And maybe he'd be right for Clove."

When Mr. Bradman came home from work the next day, Tom and Ellie rushed into the kitchen to hear the news.

"What did Mr. Miller say?" asked Tom.

Mr. Bradman was grinning.

Clove was in there, playing with a ball of wool. Her ears pricked up when she heard them talking.

"I told Mr. Miller about Bracken's litter," said Mr. Bradman. "And he started telling me all about his old cat. It seems Monty was a little rascal! Mr. Miller admitted he misses having a cat around the place — although he hadn't thought of replacing Monty."

Just then Clove decided she felt like cud-

94

dling. She ran over to Tom and rubbed her face against his ankle. Tom picked her up and she settled happily against him. She liked all the Bradmans, but especially Tom, who always seemed to have time for her.

"So is he going to take one of the kittens?" asked Tom, smiling down at Clove and scratching her under the chin.

"Well, I asked him," said Mr. Bradman, sitting down at the kitchen table. "He'd like to see them, but he hasn't made up his mind about getting one yet."

"Once he sees them, he won't be able to resist having one!" said Ellie. "When's he coming?"

"This evening," said Mr. Bradman. "Now remember, he's only said he might be interested."

"I wonder if he'll choose Clove," said Tom, stroking the top of the little kitten's head.

"But I don't want to be chosen," meowed Clove, digging her claws into Tom's sweatshirt to try and tell him. But he didn't seem to understand what she was saying. He put her down on the floor and rolled the ball of wool toward her.

When Clove heard the knock on the front door that evening, she scuttled across the kitchen floor, jumped into the cat basket, and hid behind Bracken. *Maybe they won't see me here*, thought Clove, *and then Mr. Miller might choose one of my brothers or sisters.*

Tom went to open the door to let Mr. Miller in.

"I bet all the kittens are lovely, aren't they?" Clove heard from the hallway. "I've been really looking forward to seeing them."

"Come in, Mr. Miller," Tom said. "They're all in the kitchen."

Clove peeked at the man who followed Tom into the room. He had a kind, wrinkled face, warm blue eyes, and a mop of thick white hair. Bracken got up from the basket and sidled over to him.

"Hello," Mr. Miller said, bending down to

stroke her. "You must be Bracken. What a clever cat to have nine kittens in one litter!"

"Thank you," Bracken meowed. "I'm very proud of them, but they're such a handful and they wear me out!"

Just then Amber came skidding across the kitchen floor with Emerald in pursuit.

"I'll leave you to meet them," Bracken meowed, loping back to the basket. She nudged Clove's side with her nose. "Go and say hello to Mr. Miller. He's a kind man."

Clove pretended not to hear, and when Bracken had settled herself down she snuggled into her mom's back.

Tom and Ellie had gathered the rest of Clove's brothers and sisters and placed them at Mr. Miller's feet. He laughed as he watched them. Daisy and Weed began rolling about in a play fight and Jet chased his own tail for a few minutes, then sat down and stared at Mr. Miller. Buttercup curled up in a ball and tried to go back to sleep.

"They're all beautiful," he said, and he picked each one up one at a time to have a closer look.

"Come and meet Clove," meowed Bracken loudly. "She's over here."

Clove tried to lie flat against the blanket and shut her eyes tightly. "But what's this?" she heard Mr. Miller say. Then she felt a hand petting her. "It's a little charcoal-gray kitten hiding in here."

Clove struggled as Tom lifted her out of the basket.

"Let's get a better look at you," said Mr. Miller.

Clove stared back at him. He looked friendly enough. Then she heard him sigh.

"You remind me so much of Monty," he said. "The same velvety coat, long white whiskers, and dark brown eyes."

"This one's a girl," said Tom. "She's named Clove."

"Clove," said Mr. Miller. "I like it." He

stroked her, then took her from Tom. "You've even got a fat little belly like Monty had when he was a kitten," he chuckled. "You must like your food, eh?"

"Yes, I do," purred Clove.

She felt comfortable in Mr. Miller's hands. They were gentle hands. But what Mr. Miller said next gave her a shock!

"Yes," he said to Tom and Ellie. "Your father was right. He said I'd be tempted. I can't resist this little one. If you think I'm suitable, I'd like to take Clove home."

"Great!" said Tom. "I was hoping you'd choose her — a quiet home is just what she needs. I'll get Dad."

"But I really do want to stay with my mom," Clove meowed to Tom as he left the room.

Mr. Bradman was upstairs in his study going over some bills, but he came down right away. The two men shook hands.

"Sorry, Mr. Miller," said Mr. Bradman. "I didn't realize you were here."

"He picked Clove," said Ellie. Mr. Bradman smiled.

"A good choice," he said. "When do you want to take her?"

"I could go home now and get Monty's old cat carrier," said Mr. Miller, putting Clove down on the floor. "Is that all right?"

"Yes," said Mr. Bradman, Tom, and Ellie all at once.

"No!" Clove meowed as loudly as her little voice would go. She crept into the cat basket beside Bracken.

"I don't want to go," she meowed in her mother's ear.

"Now then, dear," said Bracken as she washed Clove for the last time. "I'll miss you, too, but I can tell Mr. Miller will look after you. You'll be fine."

Half an hour later, Clove was huddled with her nose pushed into a corner of a cat carrier, riding in the back of Mr. Miller's car. Even though Bracken had told her that everything was going to be all right, Clove was worried. "I don't like the way the car moves or the noise it makes," she meowed miserably. "And I miss my mother. And this carrier doesn't smell like anyone in my family."

Suddenly, the car stopped moving and the engine stopped growling. Mr. Miller lifted the carrier out from the back of the car.

"I want to go home," meowed Clove sadly.

"Don't cry, little one," said Mr. Miller gently. "Come on, let's go inside where it's warm."

Clove watched through the holes in the carrier as Mr. Miller took her into his house. He shut the door and went to the kitchen, where he put the carrier down and undid the straps.

"Out you come," he said and gently reached inside the carrier to lift Clove out. "I'll get you a nice drink of milk."

He opened the refrigerator, got out a bottle of milk, and poured some into a saucer.

"No, thank you," Clove meowed, shying away from the saucer. "I only like water."

"Not thirsty, eh?" said Mr. Miller. "But I know just what you'd like to eat. Chicken!"

Clove watched him open the refrigerator again, take out some white stuff, cut it up on a dish, and put it down in front of her. She looked at it, sniffed it, then turned away again. She didn't like the smell of that, either.

"What? You don't want chicken?" said Mr. Miller as he picked Clove up and stroked her. "Monty used to love chicken."

"But I don't," meowed Clove.

"Oh, dear," said Mr. Miller, putting her down again. "Perhaps you're not hungry. Perhaps you want to play."

He rolled a little ball across the tiled floor. Clove watched it, but didn't chase it. The ball she'd played with at the Bradmans' house made a tinkling noise.

"Oh, dear," said Mr. Miller again. "You

won't drink, you won't eat, and you don't want to play."

Clove saw a cardboard box in the corner of the kitchen. It looked safe, so she ran over to it and jumped inside. She looked sadly up at Mr. Miller, then curled up into a gray fur ball.

The old man knelt beside the box and stroked her gently. "Well, at least you've found somewhere you seem to like," he said. "I'll get a blanket and you can sleep in there, if you prefer it to Monty's old basket."

"Yes, please," meowed Clove, "but I'm hungry and thirsty. And a bit lonely."

2

That night, Mr. Miller took the cardboard box up to his bedroom for Clove to sleep in. She hadn't touched any of the sardines, or the bits of bacon and chunks of whitefish that the old man had offered her. She was very thirsty and had forced herself to lap up some of the milk. But she really didn't like the taste. Clove tried to fall asleep despite her rumbling tummy. "I want my mom," she meowed in a tiny sad voice, "or Tom. They understand me."

Mr. Miller kept picking the kitten up, holding her gently against his chest, and stroking her. He seemed so kind, but Clove wished she could make him understand that she was hungry and still thirsty.

I just don't like all those things he's giving me, she thought. *They might have been Monty's favorite foods, but they're not mine!*

The next morning, Clove was sitting on a chair in the kitchen watching Mr. Miller eat his breakfast. Suddenly, there was a loud knock on the front door. Clove jumped down from the chair and into the cardboard box that Mr. Miller had brought downstairs.

"Grandpa!" came a high-pitched voice from outside. "It's only me!"

Who's me? wondered Clove.

"Coming, Janie!" called Mr. Miller, getting up stiffly from his chair and going to the hall.

Janie? Clove had heard that name before. Janie was a friend of Ellie's.

Clove heard Mr. Miller open the front door. "Hello, my dear," he said. "Come in."

"Mom bought you some fruit," said Janie.

"What a lucky man I am," laughed Mr. Miller. "Having a granddaughter who comes to see me every day. And she even brings me presents!"

Clove heard Janie giggle.

"And I've got something to show you!" said Mr. Miller.

"Where?" asked Janie.

"In the kitchen," said Mr. Miller.

"What is it?" giggled Janie. "Come on, Grandpa, tell me."

"It's a kitten," said Mr. Miller.

Clove heard Janie gasp.

"Oh," said Janie. "A kitten?"

"I know you didn't get along with Monty," said Mr. Miller, "but don't you even want to come and see her?" Clove thought he sounded rather disappointed.

"No!" said Janie.

Clove couldn't believe it! *Surely the girl isn't afraid of me?*

"I'll be late for school," said Janie. "I'd better run."

"All right, dear," said Mr. Miller. "But you'll come and see me after school?"

"Of course," said Janie. "Same as every day. See you later, Grandpa."

Mr. Miller came back into the kitchen shaking his head. "I'm afraid my granddaughter doesn't want to meet you just yet, little one," he said.

By the time Janie knocked on the door that afternoon, Clove still hadn't eaten anything. She had been curled up sadly in the cardboard box for most of the day. Mr. Miller kept picking her up and cuddling her. "What's wrong, little one?" he said each time.

Clove did feel better each time she was snuggled into his arms. *But how can I make him understand what I really want to eat and drink?* she thought. Mr. Miller went to let Janie in. Clove could hear them talking in the hallway again.

"Come into the kitchen, Janie dear," said her grandfather. "Come and see the kitten. I'm sure you'll love her."

"But, Grandpa . . ." said Janie. "Monty was always so mean. He used to stare at me with such a fierce frown on his face. And sometimes he'd jump on me and scratch me. He even bit me once."

Mr. Miller chuckled. "You have to remember, my dear, that when you were a very little girl, you used to tease that poor old cat all the time. You even pulled his tail. You were too young to know it would hurt and annoy him!"

"I suppose so," said Janie. "Anyway, I just don't like cats now."

Mr. Miller came back into the kitchen, leading a girl by the hand. Clove looked up at the girl. So this was Janie. She had a freckly face, green eyes, and curly red hair. She looked nice. *It was a shame she no longer liked cats*, thought Clove.

Janie stopped by the box and glanced at the kitten.

"Hello," meowed Clove in a tiny voice. "I'm Clove — and I want my mother."

"She's the same color as Monty," said Janie, turning away. "I'm thirsty." She went to get a drink of water from the tap.

"Yes, she reminds me so much of Monty when he was a kitten," said her grandfather.

Janie sat down and put her glass of water on the table. She looked at Clove, but she made no move toward the little kitten.

"I'm not like Monty," Clove meowed. "I won't hurt you."

Janie didn't seem to hear her.

"And when I saw her fat little belly I thought she'd have the same enormous appetite as Monty, but she won't eat a thing," said Mr.

Miller worriedly. "I've tried giving her all the leftovers that Monty loved. She doesn't want any of them! I keep offering her milk, but she won't drink it."

"But I don't like any of those things," meowed Clove.

"I'm beginning to worry about the poor little thing," Mr. Miller went on. "I'm thinking of phoning the Bradmans to ask their advice."

"Oh, yes," meowed Clove, leaping up and running over to Mr. Miller. "They'd tell you what I like."

Seeing Clove come nearer, Janie suddenly jumped away and knocked over her glass. Water spilled across the table and splashed onto the floor. Clove rushed over and began to eagerly lap up the water. *Lovely!* she thought as her tongue lapped faster and faster. *That's much better!*

"Thank goodness she's drinking properly at last!" Mr. Miller exclaimed, hurrying over to the sink to pour some water into a saucer. He put it down in front of Clove and watched her lap it up. "She might eat something now."

He hurried to the refrigerator and took out a small block of cheese. He cut off a small piece and offered it to Clove.

"No thank you," meowed Clove, and she jumped back into the box.

"I'd better be going now, Grandpa," said Janie.

"All right, dear," said Mr. Miller. "But tell me before you go, what do you think of my new kitten?"

Janie looked down at Clove, but she didn't smile. "Well," she said. "I suppose she's rather sweet."

Clove woke the following morning to hear Mr. Miller making strange groaning noises.

He was sitting up in bed holding his head. "Ohhhh," he moaned. "I feel terrible!"

Clove jumped out of her box and onto the

bed to look at him. His face looked very pale and his voice was raspy.

Mr. Miller looked across at her. He tried to get out of bed, but he fell back with a loud groan.

After a while, he sat up and looked at Clove again. "I'm not very well," he said. "I don't think I can get up today. Thank goodness Janie will be here soon. I can ask her to do a few things for me."

"But she doesn't like me," meowed Clove. "She might not want to come."

It wasn't long before there was the sound of a key in the lock downstairs. Mr. Miller had called his daughter to ask her to give Janie his spare front door key so that she could let herself in. Janie came upstairs after she had hung up her coat. She sat on a chair far away from Clove.

"Hello, Janie," meowed Clove.

"Well, Grandpa," said Janie, ignoring the kitten. "What do you want me to do?"

When she had gotten him a cup of tea and patted his pillows and helped him sit up, she brought the newspaper upstairs.

"Thank you, dear," said Mr. Miller.

Clove jumped over Mr. Miller's legs and buried herself under his robe that was lying on the bed. Then she pushed her way out of it and nuzzled against Mr. Miller's arm. She was

beginning to get used to him. *Perhaps he'll guess what I want to eat today*, she hoped.

"Can I get you anything else, Grandpa?" asked Janie.

"No, thanks," said Mr. Miller. "But you could play with Clove."

"I'd like that," meowed Clove.

Janie wrinkled her freckly face. "I don't know how to play with cats," she said.

"Well, could you feed her, then?" asked Mr. Miller. "See if you can persuade her to eat something."

"Yes, please!" meowed Clove.

Janie frowned at Clove, then she sighed. "All right, Grandpa," she said. "Come on, cat. Let's go downstairs."

Clove ran after Janie and soon overtook her on the stairs.

"Hey!" said Janie angrily. "Don't make me fall and break my neck."

"Sorry," meowed Clove.

They reached the kitchen and Janie opened

the refrigerator door, but all she could find were the things that her grandpa said Clove hadn't wanted to eat.

"Well," said Janie. "I'll have to go to the grocery store and buy something, I guess."

Janie knew Angie and Steve, who owned the grocery store. She grabbed her coat and ran along the street. She was out of breath when she pushed open the store door and went in. She stopped dead. A tiny black kitten stood in her way.

"Hello, Janie," called Steve from behind the counter. "Don't mind Jet. Isn't he lovely? We only got him a few days ago. I hear your grandpa's got Jet's sister, Clove."

Janie nodded as she tried to walk around Jet, but he jumped on her shoes. She stopped and looked at Steve. "Help!" she said. "I'm scared of cats."

Steve laughed. "I know Jet's large for a kitten, but he's not a monster!" he said as he lifted

Jet out of Janie's way and carried him to the back of the store.

Janie looked at the cans of cat food on the shelf. Since she didn't have much money in her wallet, she bought the cheapest one they had.

"I'd better go," she said after she'd paid for the food. "Grandpa's ill in bed and I'm his nurse for the day! And he's asked me to look after Clove!"

"Good luck!" called Steve as Janie left the shop.

Clove was waiting in the hall when Janie let herself in.

"Come on, cat," said Janie, taking off her coat and walking to the kitchen. "Let's see if you'll eat this."

Clove trotted along beside Janie, looking eagerly up at the can in her hand. "I've seen one of those cans before," she meowed.

Janie opened the can and put some into a dish.

Clove smelled a delicious and familiar smell. Her mouth began to water and her tail pointed to the ceiling, twitching excitedly. She ran around and around Janie, meowing loudly. "Hurry up! Let me get at it!"

Janie stood back and watched Clove. She gobbled up the cat food so fast the dish was soon empty.

"Grandpa!" yelled Janie. She ran into the hall and up the stairs. "Guess what!"

3

Janie ran up the stairs to tell her grandfather the good news.

"Janie!" croaked Mr. Miller when he found out what she had fed Clove. "It's too bad you had to buy that when she has all those wonderful leftovers to eat."

"But she doesn't like any of them, does she?" said Janie. "And she loves this!"

She ran downstairs again to find Clove sitting and looking at an empty dish.

"That was delicious!" Clove meowed, her tongue licking around her mouth.

"Would you like some more?" asked Janie, getting the can.

"Why not?" Clove purred loudly, then began to wolf down her second helping.

Janie crouched beside her to watch, feeling quite pleased with herself.

"This is what I ate on Liberty Street!" Clove meowed between mouthfuls.

She finished the food and licked around the dish in case she had missed any. Then she sat next to Janie and washed her face, using her front paws to make sure everything was clean. She felt so much better, now that her tummy was full.

"Thanks!" she meowed, but when she tried to nuzzle against Janie's legs, Janie backed away.

"I don't mind feeding you," said Janie, "but I don't want to pet you. You might scratch me."

Then she ran upstairs to see how her grandfather was feeling.

Clove followed her and jumped on Mr.
Miller's bed. "I feel great now!" she purred.
"How are you?"

Mr. Miller gave her a stroke. "You do look
better, little one," he whispered.

"Seeing Clove eating has made me hungry,"
said Janie. "Do you have any chips, Grandpa?"

"I always keep them especially for you,"
croaked Mr. Miller. "Help yourself."

"Thanks, Grandpa," said Janie. "Do you
want anything?"

"I'd love another cup of tea, please," Mr.
Miller replied. "Then I think I'll doze for a
while."

"Come on, then, Clove," said Janie.

Clove looked up, surprised. Then she
jumped off the bed and followed Janie downstairs. "I'm really glad you're talking to me
now," she meowed.

After taking the tea up to her grandfather,

Janie went into the den, switched on the TV, and sat down in an armchair with a bag of chips. Clove caught a whiff of them as Janie tore open the bag. She jumped up on the arm of the chair and pushed her nose as near as she dared, not wanting to make Janie nervous. Her mouth watered. She loved chips! Tom used to give them to her. "Can I have one?" she meowed.

Janie frowned and moved to another chair. Clove followed her and put out one tiny front paw to touch the bag. Janie snatched the chips away.

"Please," meowed Clove. "Just one?"

"Chips aren't for kittens," said Janie.

Clove wasn't discouraged so easily. "But I like those," she meowed. She lifted her paw again.

Janie looked at the tiny round kitten and couldn't stop herself from smiling. "I don't suppose one would hurt you," she said at last. Nervously, she held out a chip at arm's length, scared that Clove would bite her.

Very gently, Clove leaned forward and took the chip in her mouth. She crunched it, swallowed, then licked her lips. "That was good," she purred. "More, please."

Janie giggled and gave Clove another chip. Then, slowly, she reached out a hand and touched Clove's head.

Clove sat very still. "You see," she purred. "I told you I'm not at all like grumpy old Monty!"

Janie grew braver. Her hand moved down Clove's head, then over her back in a long stroke.

Clove purred louder.

Janie smiled and did it again. "You're so soft," she said. "Your coat feels like velvet."

"Thank you," purred Clove, and she pushed her head gently against Janie's hand.

"I suppose you want another chip?" Janie asked, laughing.

"Yes, please," Clove meowed happily.

*   *   *

"I've got to go home now," Janie said when the chips were finished. She picked up her coat, then ran upstairs with Clove at her heels.

Mr. Miller was sitting up in bed.

"How are you, Grandpa?" Janie asked. "I've got to go now. Mom will stop by later."

"I'm feeling a little better from that nap, thanks, dear," said Mr. Miller. Then he noticed Clove rubbing the side of her face against Janie's ankles. "Hey!" he said. "You've made a friend!"

"Oh, she's not so bad," said Janie. "And I've discovered she likes chips."

Mr. Miller chuckled. "Oh, really? Monty never showed any interest in them."

Janie bent to give her grandpa a kiss good-bye. Her long scarf dangled from her neck.

Feeling happy and playful now, Clove leaped on it, swinging back and forth. Then Clove watched as Janie put on her coat.

Mr. Miller laughed. "What a difference from earlier this morning!" he said. "It looks like you've solved Clove's problems, dear!"

"I didn't really do anything," said Janie. "I don't know anything about cats."

"Oh, yes, you do," purred Clove as she settled down to sleep on Mr. Miller's bed.

The next day, Mr. Miller felt well enough to get out of bed. The night before, Janie's mom had stopped by and given Clove the remains of the canned cat food. Now there were only leftovers from the refrigerator for her to eat.

"No, thank you," Clove meowed. "I don't like those."

After trying everything once, Mr. Miller gave up. Not long after he'd finished his own breakfast Janie arrived. She was carrying a shopping bag full of cat food. "Mom gave me the money for this," she explained.

"Thanks, dear," said Mr. Miller. "But Clove can't live on that cheap stuff! My cats have always had the best!"

Janie sighed. "Grandpa!" she said. "Clove isn't like Monty. She likes this canned food."

"She's right! I do!" meowed Clove, alarmed that Janie would have to take the canned food away again.

Janie opened one of the cans. "I've been talking to Ellie," she said. "She knows that I didn't like Monty. But she told me that every cat is different."

"I see," said Mr. Miller, smiling.

"And just because Clove looks like Monty, it doesn't mean she is going to be like him!" said Janie. "Especially if I treat her kindly."

"How about that food?" interrupted Clove.

"And Clove had canned cat food at the Bradmans'," said Janie. "It's what her mom eats. And all the kittens liked it."

"Yes, we did!" meowed Clove in her loudest voice. "So how about some for me? Now. Please!"

Janie looked down at Clove, who was almost dancing around her feet, looking up at the can.

"All right, little one," she said, spooning some food into a dish. "Grandpa was right about one thing. You have a fat little tummy because you like your food. But you like different foods than Monty."

"That's right!" meowed Clove, then she dug her head into the dish and began to eat.

Janie sat on the floor beside her as Clove ate her breakfast in record time.

When Clove had finished washing herself, Janie stroked her head and tickled her under her chin. "You're sweet, really," she said. "Maybe I'll try picking you up." Janie reached out her hands and scooped Clove into her arms.

"I like you," purred Clove.

"Look, Grandpa," Janie laughed. "I'm not frightened of her anymore!"

"And it looks as if Clove isn't frightened of you!" chuckled Mr. Miller.

On Monday morning, Mr. Bradman knocked on the back door. "It's only me, Mr. Miller," he called. "I've come to work on your orchard."

Mr. Miller opened the door. Clove was under the kitchen table, playing with a ball of string. She had recognized Mr. Bradman's voice and scampered across the room to greet him.

"Hello," said Mr. Bradman as he bent down to stroke the kitten. "Clove looks happy!"

"I am," she meowed. "I missed you all at first, but I'm all right now."

"She's eating well now," said Mr. Miller. "And we've discovered she likes chips!"

Mr. Bradman laughed. "I know where she gets that from," he said. "Our Tom loves chips. He had a soft spot for Clove and he was always sharing them with her!"

Clove rubbed her face against Mr. Bradman's legs and he bent down to scratch between her ears. "I think she's going to turn out to be a very friendly and affectionate cat," he said.

"Yes. She's settled in well now," chuckled Mr. Miller. "Thanks to Janie."

"Janie's my new friend," purred Clove.

"And Janie has overcome her fear of cats," said Mr. Miller. "Thanks to Clove!"

"Well done, Clove!" said Mr. Bradman. "Who would have thought a shy little thing like you could accomplish that!"

"Not me," meowed Clove, settling down in her cardboard box.